*Colin McNaughton*

# WATCH OUT FOR THE GIANT-KILLERS!

WALKER BOOKS
LONDON

We have not inherited the earth from our parents.
We have borrowed it from our children.

First published 1991 by Walker Books Ltd
87 Vauxhall Walk, London SE11 5HJ

© 1991 Colin McNaughton

Printed in Hong Kong by South China Printing Co. (1988) Ltd

British Library Cataloguing in Publication Data
McNaughton, Colin
Watch out for the giant-killers!
I. Title
823'.914 [J]

ISBN 0-7445-1542-4

*D*eep in the heart
of the forest something huge is
moving. Something huge and terrible.
Something green. It lumbers.
From the opposite direction
comes a small brown boy. He is hunting.
He is making his way to a clearing
where he knows he will find sweet water.
The green huge and terrible
something is also thirsty.

# "Aargh!" cried the green huge and terrible something.

# "Yeearrghh!" cried the small brown boy.

"**Ooh, you scared the life out of me, I'm shaking like a leaf,**" said the green huge and terrible something.

Good morning.

"I scared the life out of *you*! How about me?" demanded the small brown boy.

"What are you, anyway?"

"**I am a giant,**" replied the giant proudly.

"I see." But the boy didn't see at all.

"Are you a white man?" he asked.

"**No,**" said the giant. "**I am a green giant!**"

"But you must be a man. You can talk!" argued the boy.

"**All creatures can talk, my little smidgin,**" laughed the giant.

"**It's just that you don't understand their language.**"

"Sloths can't talk!" said the boy.

"**Oh, but they can! Ever so slowly,**" said the giant, ever so slowly.

"**By the time they've wished you good morning it's time for you to wish them good night!**"

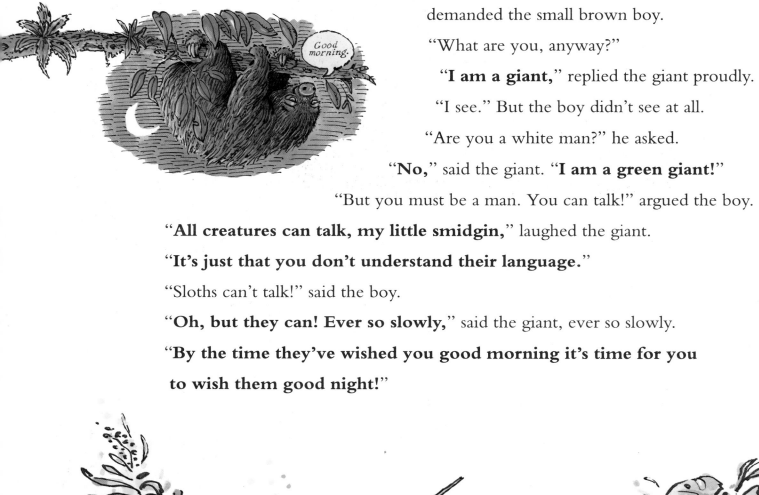

"You're very big," said the boy.

"**I'm small compared with this tree,**" replied the giant.

"But big compared with me," said the boy.

"**You are also big,**" said the giant, "**next to that snake who is about to bite your foot.**"

"Arrgh!" shouted the boy. "What snake, I don't see any snake!"

"**Just a joke,**" laughed the giant. "**A fake snake! Ha, ha!**"

"That wasn't funny," said the boy.

"**It made me laugh,**" said the giant.

"How old are you?"

"**Eighteen or nineteen hundred,**" said the giant. "**I forget.**"

"That's old," said the boy in astonishment.

"**A ripe old age,**" smiled the giant. "**How old are you?**"

"Nine," said the boy proudly. "Almost a man."

"**Now that is a remarkable coincidence,**" said the giant. "**When I was your age, I was also nine!**"

"How big were you when you were my age?" asked the boy.

"**Oh, about the same size as you are, only much bigger,**" giggled the giant.

"What do you do all day?" asked the boy.

"**I play.**"

"Play?" asked the boy.

"**You know,**" said the giant. "**I mess around – build bridges across rivers with fallen trees. Make dams in streams. Swing about in the tree tops. Make tree houses. That sort of thing.**"

"Sounds fun," said the boy.

"**It is,**" said the giant.

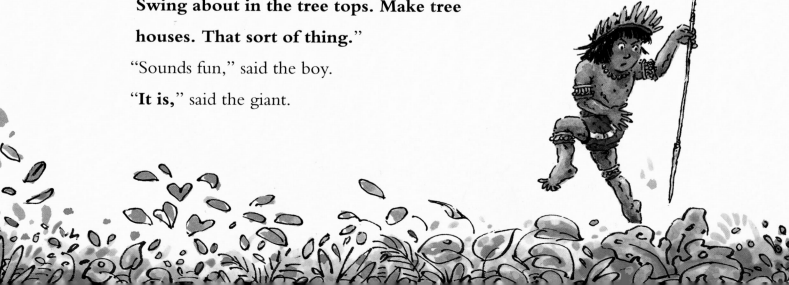

"There's a monkey on your shoulder," said the boy.

"I know," said the giant. "He thinks I'm a tree."

"You do look like a tree," said the boy.

"Thank you, young shaver. I take that as a compliment. Some of my best friends are trees."

"Where do you sleep?" asked the boy.

"If it's raining I make a hammock out of vines and sleep under the roof of the forest. If it's fine I find a nice springy tree top and just nestle in under the stars."

"What can you see from up there?" asked the boy.

"A rolling sea of green," said the giant. "Sometimes, in my dreams I swim through the tree tops."

"Would you show me?" asked the boy.

"Of course," replied the giant. "Climb on to my hand."

"There's a little tree growing on your head!" said the boy.

"Is there?" said the giant. "It must be a little nut tree! Hold on tight, we're going up."

As the giant and the boy emerged
through the roof of the forest, the giant
inhaled deeply, almost sucking a flock of
parrots into his mouth.

"**Well,**" said the giant. "**What do you think?**"

"It … it … it's the most wonderful thing I have
ever seen," stammered the boy. "But it frightens me."

"**I understand!**" said the green giant. "**It's the – *openness* of it all.
It takes your breath away.**"

"Please take me down," whispered the boy.

"This place is meant for birds, not boys."

"What do you eat?" asked the boy as they settled once more on the forest floor.

"**Berries, fruit, leaves and bark,**" said the giant.

"Bark?" said the boy.

"**Woof!**" said the giant.

"Very funny," said the boy, not amused.

"**I thought so,**" said the giant huffily.

"What is your favourite food?" asked the boy.

"**My, but you're the nosiest little sprig I've ever met!**" said the giant.

"My father said that if I don't ask I won't learn," said the boy.

"**A wise man,**" said the giant. "**I apologize. My favourite food, well, let's see. That would have to be the fruit of the Plip-plop tree. If you stand underneath the tree when the fruit is ripe, you'd think it was raining honey; it just plip-plops all over you!**"

"Don't you get all sticky?" asked the boy.

**"Of course! That's half the fun. Licking it all off!"**

"How do you normally wash yourself?" asked the boy.

**"I don't,"** said the giant.

"What, never?"

**"Not if I can help it,"** said the giant.

"Don't you smell?" asked the boy.

**"I don't know. Do I?"**

The boy sniffed.

**"Well,"** said the giant, **"what do I smell of?"**

"The forest," said the boy.

**"Best smell in the world!"**

said the giant.

"Are there other giants like you?" asked the boy.

"**There are giants all over the earth – mighty snow giants at the top and bottom of the world, mountain giants and great giants of the plains. Wherever there is wilderness it is likely that you will find a giant or two.**"

"What kind of giant are you?" asked the boy.

"**I am a forest giant,**" replied the giant. "**When I lived across the great sea some men called me 'the green man' – the spirit of the forest.**"

"How did you come to this forest?" asked the boy.

"**You really want to know?**"

The boy nodded eagerly.

"**Very well, my little seedling. Make yourself comfortable and I'll tell you my story.**"

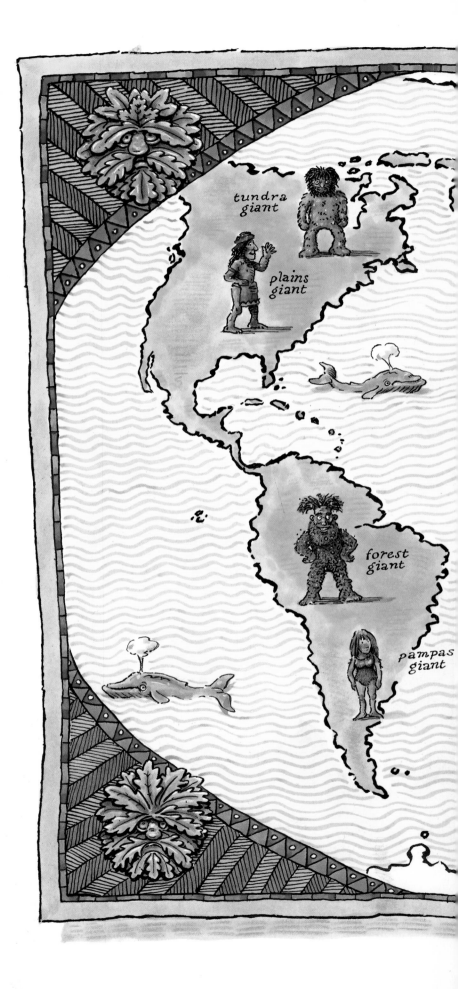

tundra giant

plains giant

forest giant

pampas giant

forest
giant

steppe
giant

desert
giant

mountain
giant

plateau
giant

savannah
giant

jungle
giant

bush
giant

outback
giant

snow
giants

N

W

E

S

"I was born on a little cluster of islands called Britain and they were very beautiful. Covered with trees from top to bottom, and from side to side. Life on the whole was grand. We giants kept ourselves to ourselves and men did likewise."

"But why did you leave such a place?"

"**Because things started to go wrong,**" said the giant. "**You see, men had always cut down trees. But that was fine, because there were few men and many trees. They cut the trees to build their houses, to fuel their fires, and to make space to plant their crops.**

an ogress

an ogret

3  4

"But the number of men just grew and grew. So they needed more and more land. That meant more and more cutting. The forest began to shrink. Of course, they never thought to replant the trees. They thought the forest would last for ever. But a man's life isn't very long, and his for-evers are an awful lot shorter than a giant's. Most of the giants retreated with the shrinking forests but some stayed where they were and that's when the real trouble started."

"What happened?" asked the boy.

"**Well, the ones who stayed were the giants called ogres,**" said the giant.

"What is an ogre?" asked the boy.

"**An ogre is a bad giant,**" said the giant.

"But why do you say these giants were bad? Surely they were brave. They didn't run away like the rest," said the boy.

"**They weren't brave,**" said the giant. "**Just as there are good and bad men, you see, there are also good and bad giants. These ogres were always looking for trouble, always up to no good, and quarrelling among themselves. Worst of all, an ogre is a giant who eats meat and his favourite kind of meat is people meat!**"

"Urrgh!" said the boy. "That's horrible."

"**Soon,**" said the giant, "**men got fed up with the ogres eating their cattle and friends and relations. And so, in the time of a King called Arthur, began the terrible days of the Giant-killers!**"

"Who were the Giant-killers?" asked the boy.

**"The Giant-killers, my little twiglet, were many and various.**

**The worst of the lot was a man named Jack. Jack the Giant-killer!"**

BLUNDERBORE · OGRE · 22'6"
DISTINGUISHING FEATURES / MOLE ON LEFT ANKLE

THUNDERDELL · OGRE · 27'8¾"
DISTINGUISHING FEATURES · YOU NAME THEM – HE'S GOT THEM!

The giant shivered at the memory. **"The first giant he killed, he**
**trapped in a pit – an ogre called Cormoran. A real nasty piece of**
**work. Everyone was glad to see the back of him.**

**"Then he slew Blunderbore who was so tall he had to go up a ladder**
**to shave himself. Then Thunderdell, then Galligantus, a hooligan**
**in yard-long boots.**

"As Jack the Giant-killer's fame grew, more and more young men set out to seek fame and fortune. The awful thing was, most of these Giant-killers didn't know the difference between a good giant and an ogre.

"Like the trees in the forest, the giants fell. One by one my friends and family died at the hands of the Giant-killers."

"How did you escape?" asked the boy.

"I just kept on the move," said the giant. "Hiding by day, travelling by night.

"At last, with most of the great forests gone, I hid on the lonely shores of the western coast. Until one day, I came face to face with none other than Jack the Giant-killer himself!

"On his belt, written in gold, were the words, 'Here's the right valiant Cornishman who slew the giant Cormoran'. Without a word, he raised his terrible sword to cut off my head.

"'Stop,' I cried. 'Why do you want to kill me?'
'Because this is the time of man,' he replied. 'And I have
promised King Arthur to rid this land of giants. So you must die!'
Now Jack, by this time, was an old man and he was not as nimble
on his feet as he once had been. As he swung his famous sword,
he lost his balance and toppled from the cliff.
Why I decided to catch him I'll never know."

"You saved him?" gasped the boy. "I would have
thrown him to the ground and stamped him flat!
Squashed him like a fly. Why didn't you kill him?"
demanded the boy.

"That's just what he asked me," said the giant.
"I said that if I was to kill him I would be
no better than he was."

"What happened then?" asked the boy.
The giant paused and lifted up his hand. "He swung his sword
again and cut off my finger," he said quietly, showing the stump.
"He did that!" cried the boy, horrified. "But you'd just saved his life.
How could he do such a horrible thing?"
"He was a man," said the giant. "Men do such things."
There was a long silence, then the boy asked,
"So what did you do then?"
"I took his sword and hurled it against
the cliff where it shattered into a
thousand pieces," said the giant.
"'Am I the last giant in Britain?'
I asked the Giant-killer.
'It is probable,' he replied.
I put him back on the cliff,
and walked into the sea."

"The sea," asked the boy, "is it like a river?"

**"A river as wide as this forest and as deep as the clouds are high,"**
replied the giant.

**"I swam for fifteen days and fifteen nights until I could swim no more.
So I turned on to my back and floated off to sleep, not caring if I ever woke
up. But wake up I did, on what seemed to be land. But the land was moving.
I was lying on the back of a whale."**

"What is a whale?" asked the boy.

**"The whale is the largest creature on earth,"** said the giant.

**"A giant of the sea. The whole world is his home. He looks like a huge fish
but is, in fact, a mammal, like you and me. For many days we talked of
giant things."**

"And you could understand his language?" asked the boy, his eyes wide.

**"We are both giants,"** said the giant simply. **"The whale told me
of the giants of the sea and I told him of the giants of the
earth. He was sad at my tale and said he had heard of
a mighty forest that would suit me down to the
ground. He had heard that the forest went
on for ever. It was pierced by a mighty
river and few men lived there."**

"The whale carried me up that mighty River Amazon for
two thousand miles into the heart of this forest.

"There we parted and here I am. That was many hundreds
of years ago and that's more words than I've spoken in all
that time put together."

"That," said the boy, "was the most amazing
story I have ever heard."

**"It was a giant story,"** said the giant.
**"There are none bigger."**

He plunged his huge green shaggy head
into the sweet-water pool and drank it dry.

**"Well, I've enjoyed our little talk, but
I must be moving on now. 'A rolling
stone gathers no moss,' y' know."**

"But where are you going?" asked the boy.
"Why don't you stay here with my people? They won't harm you."

**"Itchy feet!"** giggled the giant. **"If I stay in the same place too long I get itchy
feet and I'm very ticklish! Besides, pretty soon I'd eat up all the leaves and
you'd have a big hole in the forest and we can't have that can we? Eh?
If I stay here much longer,  I'll put down roots."**

"Will you ever come back?" asked the boy.

**"Time was,"** said the giant, **"this forest was so big I wouldn't pass the same
place more than once in a hundred years. But the cutting and burning go on
and the forest is getting smaller every day. One thing's for sure, you will be
a man if we ever meet again."**

The giant creaked to his feet, his joints cracking like burning wood.

**"Farewell, my little frond. If any giants pass this way, be kind to them."**

"Are there other giants like you in this forest?" asked the boy.

**"Oh, yes,"** said the giant, **"and ogres too, I'm afraid. So watch
your step. Well, goodbye, little sapling and good luck."**

"Goodbye, giant," said the boy. "Take care of yourself."

The giant turned
and lumbered off into
the dripping, steaming forest,
disappearing as the boy blinked.

"Watch out for the Giant-killers!"

shouted the boy into the green.
"**You too, my friend,**" came back the tiny voice
of the giant, already a long long way off.

The End